"Hey, Look! Little, tiny letters!" Sarah-Jane cried, pointing at the gravestone.

"Well, I'll be!" said the caretaker. "I never noticed them before. They're almost hidden in the rooster's feathers."

"This looks like a puzzle for the T.C.D.C.!" Timothy and Titus exclaimed.

THE MYSTERY OF THE

GRAVESTONE RIDDLE

Elspeth Campbell Murphy
Illustrated by Chris Wold Dyrud

Chariot Books
David C. Cook Publishing Co.

A Wise Owl Book
Published by Chariot Books,
an imprint of David C. Cook Publishing Co.
David C. Cook Publishing Co., Elgin, Illinois 60120
David C. Cook Publishing Co., Weston, Ontario

The Mystery of the Gravestone Riddle
© 1988 by Elspeth Campbell Murphy for text and Chris Wold
Dyrud for illustrations

Cover design by Chris Patchel
First Printing, 1988
Printed in the United States of America
93 92 91 90   5 4

Library of Congress Cataloging-in-Publication Data
Murphy, Elspeth Campbell.
   The mystery of the gravestone riddle.

   (The Ten Commandments mysteries)
   Summary: When three cousins solve a 100-year-old murder, they
learn about the commandment forbidding killing.
   [1. Cousins—Fiction. 2. Mystery and detective stories. 3. Ten
commandments—Fiction.]
I. Dyrud, Chris Wold, ill. II. Title. III. Series:
Murphy, Elspeth Campbell. Ten Commandments mysteries.
PZ7.M95316Myc   1988   [FIC]   87-16721
ISBN 1-55513-800-4

"You shall not murder."

Exodus 20:13 (NIV)

CONTENTS

1
AT THE CEMETERY

The three cousins, Timothy, Titus, and Sarah-Jane, were having an argument about whether cemeteries were scary or not.

Timothy said they weren't the least bit scary.

Titus said they were scary if you were all by yourself.

And Sarah-Jane said they were scary only at night.

The cousins were arguing about cemeteries because they were walking through one.

Fortunately, it was a bright, summer evening, and Sarah-Jane's father was with them.

They pushed through the big, iron gates into the old part of the graveyard, where all the fancy statues were.

"Hey, neat-O!" said Timothy softly. "I've

never seen anything like *this* before!''

Sarah-Jane's father said, "That's because the suburb where you live, Timothy, was just farmland a hundred years ago. But Fairfield is an old, country town that goes way back—more than a hundred years."

Timothy was visiting Sarah-Jane from the suburbs.

And Titus was visiting Sarah-Jane from the city.

It was a good time for them to be in Sarah-Jane's town, because Fairfield was celebrating. Its library was one hundred years old!

The children in Fairfield had all picked projects to do for the celebration. Timothy and Titus were helping Sarah-Jane with her project.

Sarah-Jane was going to make a gravestone rubbing. First she would tape a piece of tracing paper on a gravestone. Then she would rub the paper with a piece of charcoal. When she took the paper away, she would have a copy of the words and pictures on the gravestone.

Sarah-Jane's eyes were shining, and she could hardly stand still.

10

"I can't *wait* for Library Day!" she cried. "All the kids are going to dress up in old-time costumes.

"Of course, that dumb Nicole Manning is bragging to everybody that the dress her grandmother is making her is going to be *so-o-o beautiful!* Ha!

"Anyway, we'll all stand beside our projects in the new Children's Room. And there will be punch and cookies. People will come around to see what we made. And—and this will be the best super-duper project ever!"

"Now, hold on, Sarah-Jane," said her father when she stopped to take a breath. "You haven't even made your gravestone rubbing yet. And Library Day is the day after tomorrow. You're getting a late start."

Sarah-Jane explained to Timothy and Titus, "That's because Miss Amelia Featherstone wouldn't let me interview her.

"See—at first my project was going to be writing a story for the newspaper about the old days. But Miss Featherstone didn't want to talk about them. I wonder why not?"

"I don't know," said her father. "That puzzled me, too."

"Maybe Miss Featherstone has a secret she's trying to hide!" said Timothy.

"Maybe," said Sarah-Jane. "But, anyway, I have a new project now. The librarian told us that a long time ago people didn't know as much about medicine. So lots of times babies got sick and died. I want to find a gravestone for a poor, sweet, little baby."

"OK," said Titus. "Now we know what to look for."

12

2
COPYCATS

They had just started to look when an angry voice said, "Sarah-Jane Cooper! What are *you* doing here?"

Sarah-Jane whirled around as a girl stepped out from behind a big, shady tree.

"I could ask *you* the same question, Nicole Manning!" said Sarah-Jane.

"I'm doing my Library Day project," said Nicole.

"You can't do gravestone rubbings," said Sarah-Jane. "Because that's what *I'm* doing. You're just copying."

"No way!" said Nicole. "*I* got here *first*! See?"

She held out several finished rubbings.

Sarah-Jane looked at them and yelled, "Did

13

you take all the babies, Nicole Manning?!"

"No," said Nicole. "But even if you do grave-stone rubbings, you'd better not do *baby* grave-stones! Because then you would be copying me. Copycat! Copycat! And my costume will be better than yours, too!"

Nicole ran off, and Sarah-Jane sank down under the tree.

"I HATE that stupid Nicole!" she muttered.

"That's enough, Sarah-Jane!" said her father. "No one says you have to be best friends with Nicole. You don't even have to play with her. But I don't want to hear *anymore* of that hate talk! Is that clear?"

"Yes, sir."

Sarah-Jane stared down at the bumpy roots of the tree. It was embarrassing to be yelled at in front of your cousins.

"All right," said her father. " Now get up, and we'll go look around some more."

When Sarah-Jane's dad was a little ways off, Timothy whispered, "S-J, who was that kid?"

"Oh, just some dumb girl who was in my class last year. The teacher said we shouldn't be in the same room again this fall.''

"Wow!" said Titus. "Is Nicole your enemy or something?"

"I guess so," said Sarah-Jane. "One time we even got grounded for fighting. But *she started it*!"

"So—are you still going to do a gravestone rubbing?" asked Timothy.

Sarah-Jane sighed. "Yes, but now it won't be as special." She brightened up a little. "At least the three of us will have neat costumes. Better than Nicole's!"

Timothy and Titus looked at each other.

Timothy said, "Uh, Sarah-Jane? We don't know how to break this to you. But there's *no way* we're going to wear those costumes your mom is making. No way, José!"

"WHAT!?" yelled Sarah-Jane.

Titus said, "Calm down, S-J! Maybe—just maybe—one of us *might* wear a sailor suit. But not that Fauntle-thing!"

"Fauntleroy," said an old woman. She looked up with a smile from the family graves where she was pulling weeds.

"Miss Featherstone!" said Sarah-Jane. "I didn't even see you down there. I'd like you to meet my cousins. This is Timothy Dawson and Titus McKay."

"How do you do?" said the old lady. "I quite understand your feelings about the Fauntleroy costume, boys. But that style was very popular a hundred years ago when my father, John-Henry, was a boy about your age."

"How did anyone ever *think up* clothes like

that?'' asked Titus.

Miss Featherstone laughed. "Little Lord Fauntleroy was a character in a children's book. And people liked him so much, they copied the clothes he was wearing from a drawing in the book.

"My father's aunt bought my father a Fauntleroy suit. It had velvet, knee-length pants that you wore with tights. It had a big, lace collar and a pink, satin sash. And to go with it, there was a big, wide hat with a long fluffy feather.''

"Yeah—That's it exactly!'' cried Timothy.

"YUCKY!"

"BEAUTIFUL!" cried Sarah-Jane.

Titus asked, "Did John-Henry—your dad—have to wear that suit all the time?"

He plopped down beside Miss Featherstone and began pulling weeds. Timothy and Sarah-Jane did the same.

"The suit was only for parties," said Miss Featherstone. Her eyes twinkled. "But my father wore it only once. First, he 'accidentally' fell down in a mud puddle. Then, he 'accidentally' crawled under a thornbush. And after that, the suit was so stained and torn, he couldn't wear it again."

"Smart kid!" said Timothy.

"Yes!" said Miss Featherstone with a chuckle. But suddenly she looked sad.

Sarah-Jane said, "Is something wrong, Miss Featherstone?"

The old lady smiled gently at her and said, "Oh, my dear child. I *do* owe you an apology. You must have thought it odd of me not to help you with your story for the newspaper."

Sarah-Jane's father joined them. He said,

18

"Does something about Library Day bother you, Miss Featherstone?"

"Yes," said Miss Featherstone. "Something that happened a hundred years ago."

Miss Featherstone continued, "I was hoping no one would dig up the old newspaper stories about my grandfather. But, of course, they did. People want to know about the past. And that's especially true, now that all those old books and papers have been found in the library basement."

"Can you tell us your secret?" asked Timothy.

"Soon everyone will know," said Miss Featherstone. "So I will tell you what happened.

"My father, John-Henry Featherstone, was an only child, and his mother had died when he was born. So—it was just John-Henry and his father, Charles.

"John-Henry was about the same age as you children when the people of Fairfield made plans to build a library.

"John-Henry's father, Charles Featherstone, (my grandfather) was in charge of collecting the money the people raised for the library.

"One morning, John-Henry came back from visiting his aunt overnight. And he was surprised to find that his father wasn't home—and his father's horse was gone.

"Then later, some townspeople found my grandfather's horse running loose. They were afraid that Charles might have fallen off and hurt himself. So they searched for him. And, sure enough, they found him—at the bottom of a steep hill. But they couldn't help him. He was already dead."

"Poor John-Henry!" exclaimed Timothy. "I couldn't *stand it* if *my* father died!"

"It was even worse than you think, Timothy," said Miss Featherstone. "The horse's saddlebags were stuffed with money—the library's money."

The cousins stared at her in silence for a moment. At last Titus said, "You mean—your grandfather *stole* the library's money? And he was leaving town with it?"

Miss Featherstone nodded sadly. "That's what

everyone said, Titus. But my dad, John-Henry, never believed it. John-Henry knew that his father would never steal or go off and leave him.''

Sarah-Jane asked, ''What happened to John-Henry?''

''He went to live with his aunt. She was very good to him.'' Miss Featherstone winked at Timothy and Titus. ''Except for the time she made him wear that Fauntleroy suit.''

Sarah-Jane's father asked, ''Who took charge of the library money after your grandfather died, Miss Featherstone?''

''A Mr. Samuel Higgins,'' said Miss Featherstone, as Mr. Cooper helped her to her feet and the kids picked up her gardening tools. ''I always heard stories when I was growing up about how Mr. Higgins and my grandfather quarreled all the time. They couldn't get along at all.

''But strangely enough, Mr. Higgins became quiet and sad after my grandfather Charles died.

''Sam Higgins did a good job as library treasurer. But people said he kept to himself. He never smiled. I think you'll find his gravestone here in the old part of the cemetery somewhere.''

"What kind of gravestone is it?" asked Sarah-Jane, looking around at the carved angels and flowers.

"I don't know," said Miss Featherstone. "But I imagine it's rather plain. Mr. Higgins didn't have any close relatives. So he wouldn't have a special gravestone—not unless he planned it himself ahead of time."

They waved good-bye to Miss Featherstone and went to look for Sam Higgins's grave.

5

SAM HIGGINS'S GRAVESTONE

When they found the grave, they saw that the marker wasn't plain at all. First, there was a short, stone pillar. And on top of the pillar there was a big, stone cushion with tassles. And on top of the cushion there was a big, open, stone Bible.

They walked around the gravestone to see if there were Bible words carved into the page. But to their surprise, all they saw was a picture—of a *rooster*!

The cousins were wondering about this when Sarah-Jane's father reminded them it was getting late.

Sarah-Jane said, "OK. I just decided to do Mr. Higgins's gravestone for my project, Daddy. After all, he helped start the library. Too bad Nicole didn't think of that!"

"Sarah-Jane!"

"Sorry, Daddy."

They set to work. It was hard, because they had to be careful and fast at the same time.

They were just finishing when the caretaker came by. "I have to lock the gates now," he said.

"See the rubbing we made?" asked Sarah-Jane, as she cleaned the charcoal off her hands with a Wash 'n' Dry.

"Very nice work," said the caretaker. "I've always thought the Higgins gravestone had an interesting picture symbol."

"What do you mean?" asked Timothy.

The caretaker explained. "Well, sometimes the pictures on gravestones are just for decoration. But a lot of times the pictures *mean* something."

The cousins and Sarah-Jane's dad gathered up their stuff. The caretaker walked with them to the gate. He pointed to a gravestone that had a picture of an hourglass with wings.

"There now," he said. "What do you think *that* picture means?"

Titus took a wild guess. "Time flies?"

The caretaker laughed. "Exactly! That picture is a way of saying that we each have only one lifetime. And we should use our time well."

Sarah-Jane asked, "What about the rooster on Mr. Higgins's gravestone?"

The caretaker answered by asking *them* a question. "Do you know the Bible story about Jesus' disciple Peter and a rooster?"

"Hey, yeah!" cried Timothy. "I remember that one! Jesus was going to be crucified. And Peter said he would stick with him. But Jesus said, 'No, you won't, Peter. Before the rooster crows today, you will lie three times and say you don't even know Me!' "

"Yes!" said Titus. "And that's exactly what Peter did. Then Peter heard the rooster crowing, and he remembered what Jesus had said. Peter was *really sorry*!"

"And Jesus forgave him," said Sarah-Jane.

"Right," said the caretaker. "That's why a rooster on a gravestone stands for sin and forgiveness."

"You mean Mr. Higgins did something really wrong?" asked Titus. "Is that what he wanted people to know when they looked at his gravestone—that he was sorry and that God forgave him?"

Timothy added, "Everybody does wrong things—but maybe what Mr. Higgins did was something *really serious*!"

"Like what?" asked Sarah-Jane.

The caretaker shrugged. "I have no idea."

Sarah-Jane took a closer look at the rubbing. Suddenly she cried, "Hey, look! Little, tiny letters!"

6
THE MYSTERIOUS RIDDLE

"Well, I'll be!" said the caretaker. "I never noticed them before. They're almost hidden in the rooster's feathers."

But the letters were there all right:
EX XX XIII MARK.

Mr. Cooper said, "Some of them might be Roman numerals. .... This looks like a puzzle for the T.C.D.C.!"

"What's a 'teesy-deesy'?" asked the caretaker.

"It's letters," Sarah-Jane explained to him.
"Capital T.
Capital C.
Capital D.
Capital C.
It stands for the Three Cousins Detective Club."

The caretaker nodded. "Well, good luck with your gravestone riddle!"

The T.C.D.C. wanted to work on the riddle as soon as they got home. But Sarah-Jane's mom (the boys' Aunt Sue) wanted them to try on their costumes. So Timothy and Titus hid in the bathroom. And they wouldn't come out until Aunt Sue promised they could *both* wear sailor suits.

"But what about the Fauntleroy suit?" cried Sarah-Jane. "It's *so beautiful,* with all that velvet and lace and satin and feathers!"

"If you like it so much, *you* wear it!" said

Titus.

"I already have a costume," said Sarah-Jane.

But they didn't want to waste time arguing. They had a riddle to solve.

Sarah-Jane's father gave them a chart for figuring out Roman numerals. There was no EX on the chart, so they skipped that and went on to XX.

Titus said, "X means 10. So two X's means 20."

They moved on to the next part. Timothy said, "X means 10, and I means one. So XIII means 13."

"OK," said Sarah-Jane. "That takes care of the Roman numerals. So now we have EX 20 13 MARK. What does EX mean? The gravestone had an open Bible on it. Maybe it has something to do with the Bible. . . ."

"EXodus!" cried Timothy and Titus together.

"I think you're right, Tim and Ti!" said Sarah-Jane. "And you know what else? I think 20 is the chapter number! And 13 is the verse number!"

Titus said, "Exodus, chapter 20, is where the Ten Commandments are. I wonder if verse 13 is a commandment?''

Sarah-Jane ran to get her Bible. They were so excited, they could hardly turn the pages.

They read the words silently. Then their mouths dropped open in amazement. Exodus 20:13 gave them the sixth commandment—*You shall not murder.*

7
THE SEARCH

At last Sarah-Jane said in a voice squeaky from shock, "Do you think Mr. Higgins *killed* somebody?"

Timothy said, "Maybe that's the sin he was sorry for. Maybe that's what the rooster means."

"Did he kill somebody named Mark?" asked Titus.

Timothy and Sarah-Jane looked at him in surprise. They had almost forgotten the last word of the riddle.

Timothy said, "Mark is another book of the Bible. But there are no chapter or verse numbers after the word *Mark* in the riddle."

Sarah-Jane said, "Or maybe *Mark* isn't someone's name. Maybe it's like when you *make a mark* with a pencil—or when you use a *bookmark*."

Titus said excitedly, "I wonder if Mr. Higgins *marked* Exodus 20:13 in his Bible? I wonder if there's another clue there—in his Bible?"

"But how could we ever find his Bible?" asked Timothy. "Where could we even look?"

Sarah-Jane sighed and said, "The only place I know where they found old books and stuff was in the library basement. . . ."

The three cousins stared at one another. Then all at the same time they jumped up and ran to get Sarah-Jane's parents.

Sarah-Jane's mother called the librarian, who was a friend of hers.

When she got off the phone she said, "I have some good news and some bad news.

"The good news is that they *did* find boxes of books and papers that belonged to Samuel Higgins. The president of the historical society has them at his house for sorting."

"So what's the bad news?" asked Sarah-Jane.

Mrs. Cooper looked right at her. "The president of the historical society is Mr. Manning—Nicole's father."

"Oh, NO!!!" cried Sarah-Jane, falling on the sofa.

"That's right," said her mother. "If you want to solve this riddle, you have to go over to Nicole's house and be nice to her and let her help you."

Sarah-Jane just groaned and pulled a pillow over her head.

"Come on, S-J!" pleaded Timothy.

"This is important!" cried Titus.

Nicole was catching fireflies outside her house when Mr. Cooper and the cousins arrived.

She waited until Sarah-Jane's father was half-way up the front walk before she said, "Sarah-Jane Cooper! What are *you* doing here?"

"Every time you see me you ask me that," complained Sarah-Jane.

"Don't start fighting!" said Timothy. "We have work to do."

Titus said, "We're solving a mystery, Nicole, and you can help us."

Nicole looked at Sarah-Jane as if she couldn't believe it.

34

"It's true, Nicole," said Sarah-Jane. "We have to find Sam Higgins's Bible. Your dad said we could look through the library boxes."

"OK, I'll help," said Nicole.

And after they had looked for a long time, it was Nicole who found the Bible.

"Turn to Exodus!" cried Sarah-Jane. "There might be a bookmark there!"

But there was more than a bookmark. There was an envelope.

8

PERSONAL AND CONFIDENTIAL

The envelope was yellow with age. It was sealed shut with a spot of wax that had never been broken open. On the front of the envelope there was faded writing that said:

To be opened after my death.
PERSONAL AND CONFIDENTIAL
To John-Henry Featherstone.

"But that's Miss Featherstone's father," said Sarah-Jane. "And he died a long time ago."

"Then his daughter should be the one to open it," said Nicole's father.

So they all took the letter to Miss Amelia Featherstone.

Miss Featherstone's hands were shaking with excitement as she broke the seal. She asked Sarah-Jane's father to read the letter aloud.

My dear John-Henry,
This is the hardest letter I have ever had to write. And it will probably be my last, because I am ill and won't live much longer. This letter will be hard for you to read, too, because it will tell you that I killed your father.

Everyone gasped. Miss Featherstone's eyes filled with tears. But she motioned for Sarah-Jane's father to go on reading.

Please believe me, John-Henry, when I tell you that I never meant to harm your father, Charles. I'm sure you know we were always quarreling. The truth is—we never even tried to get along.

Sarah-Jane and Nicole glanced at each other and then stared down at the carpet.

We met one evening by chance, and, as usual, a quarrel broke out. It doesn't matter now what it was about. I lost my temper, and I pushed Charles. He slipped and fell down the hill. He hit his head on a rock and died.
I panicked. I thought people might find out what had happened. So I got the idea to make it

look as if his horse threw him. I took your father's keys and went back to the house. You were visiting your aunt then, remember?

I knew your father was going to take the library money to the bank the next day—but that it was still in a locked box in his study. So I put the money in the horse's saddlebags. And then I led the horse back to the hill and turned him loose.

I figured people would be so upset about the stolen money, they wouldn't wonder too much about how your father fell.

Sarah-Jane's father stopped to clear his throat.

"Then what happened?" asked Nicole.

"Keep reading, Daddy," said Sarah-Jane.

"Hurry up," said Timothy and Titus.

And I was right. No one suspected a thing.

In fact, the townspeople asked me to take over as treasurer for the library. I did the best job I could.

I know people think I am odd. They think I am a lonely and sad old man. And they are right. But they don't know why I am the way I am. I have lived for many years with this terrible secret.

But now I have come to believe that God loves

me. He forgives me. Tomorrow I am going to see the stonecutter. I have a good idea for what I want him to put on my gravestone.

When you read this letter, and see my gravestone, you will understand, John-Henry. How I wish I had the courage to tell you all this in person! But after I am gone, they will find this letter and give it to you.

Oh, John-Henry, your papa was not a thief. He did not go off and leave you when you were a little boy. He died because of me. Forgive me. Please forgive me.

Yours very sorrowfully, Samuel Higgins.

All of them sat in silence for a long time.

9

A CRIME FORGIVEN

Then Titus asked quietly, "Why didn't John-Henry ever get the letter?"

Nicole's father said, "We'll never know for sure, Titus. Mr. Higgins didn't have any relatives. So someone else must have packed up his things after he died. Probably someone just shoved this Bible in a box with his other books—without even noticing the envelope."

Timothy said, "Do you think John-Henry ever noticed the gravestone riddle and figured out what it meant?"

"He may have," said Mr. Manning. "But we'll never know that, either."

Sarah-Jane asked, "Miss Featherstone, do you think John-Henry would have forgiven Mr. Higgins?"

Miss Featherstone looked out into the darkness. At last she said in a faraway voice, "It would have been a very hard thing to do—to forgive someone for killing your father. But, yes—with God's help—John-Henry would have forgiven Sam Higgins."

Miss Featherstone asked Mr. Manning to give the letter to the newspaper. Then she quietly hugged each of them.

The dads and the kids walked together down the street.

"Well," Mr. Manning said. "I'm glad that old story about Charles Featherstone stealing the library money will be cleared up in time for Library Day."

"Library Day!" groaned Nicole, as if she had a stomachache.

"What's the matter?" asked Timothy.

"I thought you were looking forward to Library Day," said Titus.

"What about your neat costume?" asked Sarah-Jane (not at all snottily).

"My costume is the problem," wailed Nicole. "My grandma was making it. But she called a little while ago. Grandma has the flu! My dress is nowhere near finished! And my mom doesn't sew!"

"Can you come to my house?" asked Sarah-Jane suddenly. "I have a costume you can use."

Nicole tried on Sarah-Jane's dress. Sarah-Jane tried on the Fauntleroy suit. Together they looked in the mirror. "FABULOUS!" they said.

They ran downstairs to show everyone. When

Timothy saw them he said, "S-J! You look just like a girl!"

"I *am* a girl," said Sarah-Jane.

"I know," said Timothy. "But in those boys' clothes you *really* look like a girl."

Sarah-Jane thought about that. "But if these are boys' clothes, how come I don't look like a boy?"

Titus said, "We figured out the gravestone riddle, but we'll never figure *this* out!"

So they didn't even try.

The End

THE TEN COMMANDMENTS MYSTERIES

When Timothy, Titus, and Sarah-Jane, the three cousins, get together the most ordinary events turn into mysteries. So they've formed the T.C.D.C. (That's the Three Cousins Detective Club.)

And while the three cousins are solving mysteries, they're also learning about the Ten Commandments and living God's way.

You'll want to solve all ten mysteries along with Sarah-Jane, Ti, and Tim:

The Mystery of the Laughing Cat—"You shall not steal." *Someone stole rare coins. Can the cousins find the thief?*

The Mystery of the Messed-up Wedding—"You shall not commit adultery." *Can the cousins find the missing wedding ring?*

The Mystery of the Gravestone Riddle—"You shall not murder." *Can the cousins solve a 100-year-old murder case?*

The Mystery of the Carousel Horse—"You shall not covet." *Why does the stranger want an old, wooden horse?*

The Mystery of the Vanishing Present—"Remember the Sabbath day and keep it holy." *Can the cousins figure out who has Grandpa's missing birthday gift?*

The Mystery of the Silver Dolphin—"You shall not give false testimony." *Who's telling the truth—and who's lying?*

The Mystery of the Tattletale Parrot—"You shall not misuse the name of the Lord your God." *What will the beautiful green parrot say next?*

The Mystery of the Second Map—"You shall have no other gods before me." *Can the cousins discover who dropped the strange map?*

The Mystery of the Double Trouble—"Honor your father and your mother." *How could Timothy be in two places at once?*

The Mystery of the Silent Idol—"You shall not make for yourself an idol." *If the idol could speak, what would it tell the cousins?*

Available at your local Christian bookstore.

David C. Cook Publishing Co., Elgin, IL 60120

SHOELACES AND BRUSSELS SPROUTS

One little lie, but BIG trouble!

When Alex lies to her mom about losing her shoelaces, it doesn't seem like a big deal. But how do you replace special baseball laces when you don't have any money and you're not allowed to go to the store alone? A big softball game is coming up, and Alex knows the coach won't let her pitch in shoes without laces—or in cowboy boots!

Every kid gets into the predicaments that Alex does—ones that start out small and mushroom. Readers will learn from Alex's mistakes and understand that they have the same sources of help that she turns to: A God who loves them and wants to help them, and parents who understand.

Other books in the Alex Series . . .

2 *French Fry Forgiveness*—Sometimes making friends is harder than making enemies.

3 *Hot Chocolate Friendship*—Is winning first place as important to Alex as being a friend?

4 *Peanut Butter and Jelly Secrets*—Obeying her parents (even in little things) beats the awful results of disobeying.

Available at your local Christian bookstore.

David C. Cook Publishing Co.
850 N. Grove Ave.
Elgin, IL 60120

Chariot Books